But all of th
were so annoying
that princess Freya
fed them to her
dragon.

the end

THIS DOESN'T
LOOK EVIL
ANYWAY
♡

Wally & Freya

by Lindsey Pointer

illustrated by Stella Mongodi

Good Books

New York, New York

dedication

this book belongs to:

For Fern, Charlie, and all the little peacemakers. —LP

Wally was a bully.
That's what everybody said.
They were sure that hurtful thoughts
were all that *filled* his head.

Wally stole lunch every day
from Bella Jo the bear, and he
always hogged the crayons
and then refused to even share.

Needless to say, when it was time
for the kids to play,
Wally's classmates all would holler,
"Wally, go away!"

During recess, kids brought pens
and imaginations soared.
They wrote of pirates, goblins, ghouls,
dragons, knights, and lords.

Freya the red fox wrote
the most captivating tales
of terrifying monsters with
big teeth as sharp as nails.

One day, Freya's book of tales
simply disappeared.
"It's lost and gone *forever!*"
or so the children *feared.*

Raphael the rabbit
spoke up *fast* to save the day.
"Wally took the book," he said.
"Quick! He went that way!"

Chasing after Wally,
  they were shocked by what they found.
Pages of her book were scattered
  all across the ground.

Freya's words were hidden
under Wally's scary doodles
of terrifying monsters eating
eyes and guts like noodles.

They all let out a gasp. "What have you
    done?" the group exclaimed.
Wally ran into the forest,
    looking quite ashamed.

But Freya thought twice
    as she watched young Wally go
and followed down the grassy path
    to where the oak trees grow.

Wally was there, hanging his head
and kicking the dirt.
Freya saw in Wally's eyes
that both of them felt hurt.

"Your drawings are amazing!"
Freya genuinely said.
This made Wally smile, and
he slowly turned his head.

"Why'd you take my book?" she asked
    with kindness in her eyes.
"I don't know," said Wally,
    letting out a big long sigh.

"I guess I just always wanted
    to be part of the fun.
But you wouldn't understand;
    you're friends with everyone."

"Nobody likes me," Wally said
while looking very sad.
"Sometimes I get so sad, and then
that sadness makes me mad!"

He told his new *friend* Freya
about troubles in his home,
and told her how he *felt* so scared
and completely alone.

Freya sat and listened, and
she let Wally talk on,
and by the end of Wally's story,
her anger was gone.

"I have a *fun* idea," she said
with kindness in her smile,
and together they gathered her book's
pages in a pile.

The next day, the
kids gathered by the
biggest old oak tree.
What they *found* when
they arrived was
quite the sight to see.

Wally's illustrations were
   all pinned up on the bark,
scary drawings of mean monsters
   and terrible sharks.

Freya told a story and
it made them come alive;
the monsters were embarking on
a dangerous deep-sea dive.

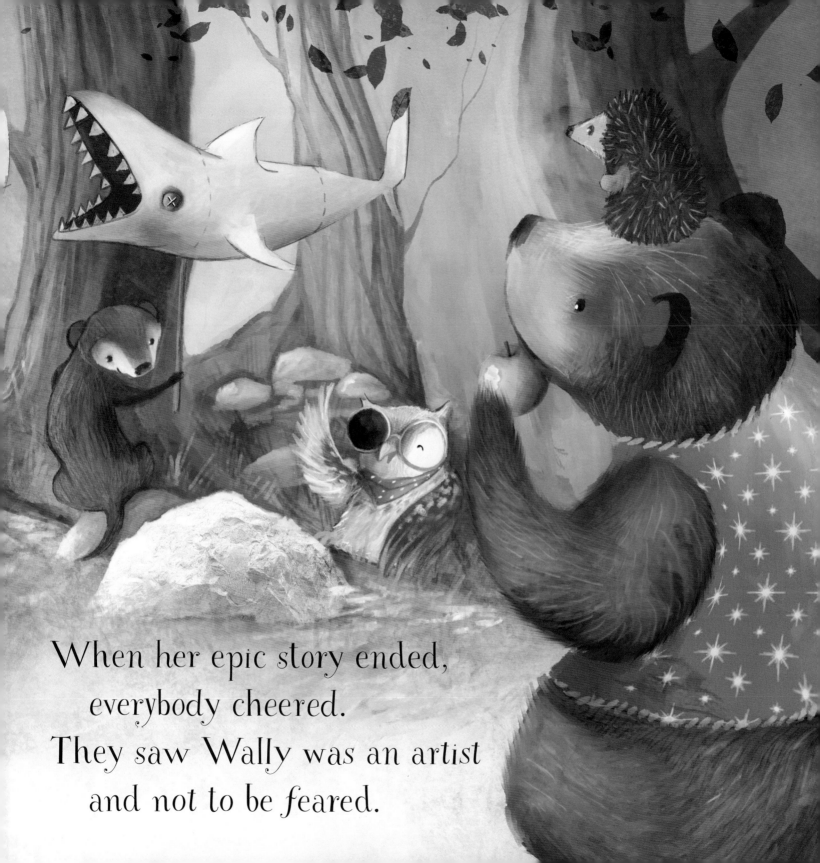

When her epic story ended,
everybody cheered.
They saw Wally was an artist
and not to be *feared*.

From that day on, Wally was
a member of the crew.
The others wrote the stories,
and as for Wally?
He drew!

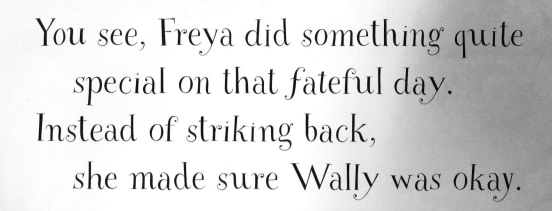

You see, Freya did something quite
special on that *fateful* day.
Instead of striking back,
she made sure Wally was okay.

There is always much more to people than we can see. Beautiful things happen when we practice empathy.

Good Books books may be purchased in bulk at special discounts for sales promotion, corporate gifts, fund-raising, or educational purposes. Special editions can also be created to specifications. For details, contact the Special Sales Department, Good Books, 307 West 36th Street, 11th Floor, New York, NY 10018 or info@skyhorsepublishing.com.

Good Books is an imprint of Skyhorse Publishing, Inc.®, a Delaware corporation.

Visit our website at www.goodbooks.com.

10 9 8 7 6 5 4 3 2

Library of Congress Cataloging-in-Publication Data is available on file.

Cover design by David Ter-Avanesyan
Cover illustration by Stella Mongodi

Print ISBN: 978-1-68099-791-0
Ebook ISBN: 978-1-68099-834-4

Printed in China